THE ADVENTURES OF
THOR

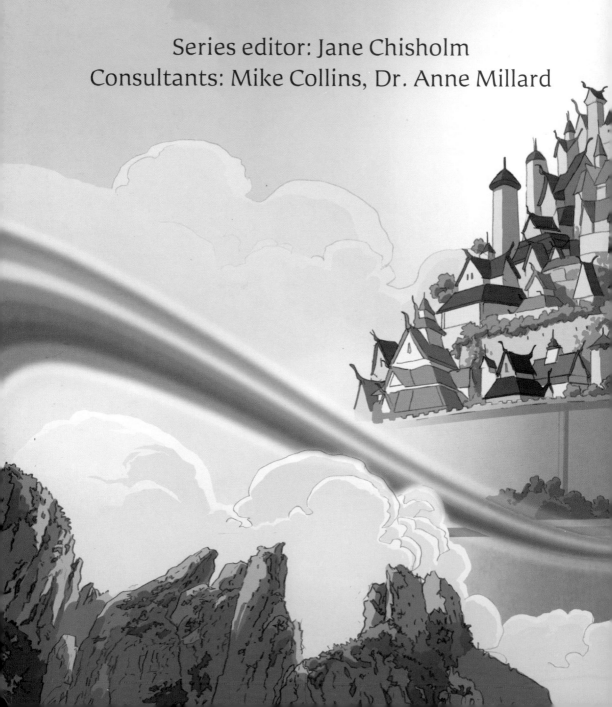

Retold by Russell Punter

Illustrated by Andrea da Rold

Series editor: Jane Chisholm
Consultants: Mike Collins, Dr. Anne Millard

THE ADVENTURES OF
THOR

The Nine Realms

This map shows the nine realms in which Thor's adventures take place.

Asgard
Realm of the Aesir
– home to the Aesir leader, Odin, his son, Thor, and their fellow warrior gods.

YGGDRASIL
The world tree

Midgard
Realm of the mortals
– surrounded by an ocean, inhabited by the great sea serpent Jörmungandr.

Jötunheimr
Realm of the giants
– home to, among others, Thrymr – king of the frost giants, Utgard-Loki and his kingdom of Utgard, as well as Hrungnir, Hymir and Geirröd.

Niflheim
Realm of the dead
– a misty, frozen world, home to those who failed to die a heroic or notable death.

– Yggdrasil's branches reach out all over the world and into the sky. The three roots which support the tree lead to Asgard, Jötunheimr and Niflheim.

Vanaheim
Realm of the Vanir
– the Vanir warrior Freyr and his sister Freya came from here before being made honorary members of the Aesir.

Alfheim
Realm of the Light Elves
– home to the Light Elves who are fairer than the sun.

Svartalfheim
Realm of the Dark Elves
–the sons of Ivaldi are Dark Elves, closely related to dwarves.

Nithavellir
Realm of the dwarves
– the brothers Brokkr and Sindri are dwarves.

Muspelheim
Realm of the fire giants
– a land of scorching flames, home to Surtur, leader of the destructive fire giants.

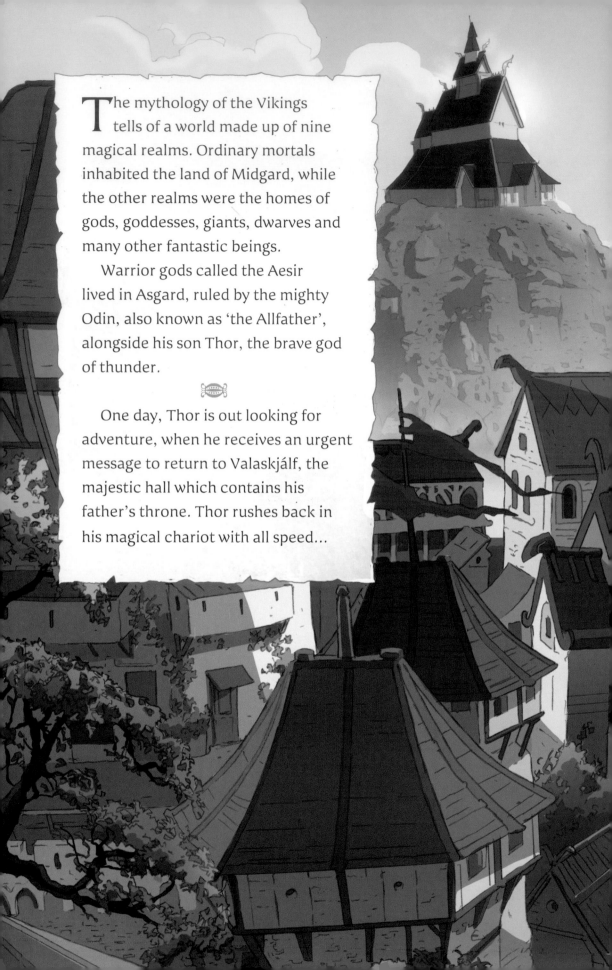

The mythology of the Vikings tells of a world made up of nine magical realms. Ordinary mortals inhabited the land of Midgard, while the other realms were the homes of gods, goddesses, giants, dwarves and many other fantastic beings.

Warrior gods called the Aesir lived in Asgard, ruled by the mighty Odin, also known as 'the Allfather', alongside his son Thor, the brave god of thunder.

One day, Thor is out looking for adventure, when he receives an urgent message to return to Valaskjálf, the majestic hall which contains his father's throne. Thor rushes back in his magical chariot with all speed...

AND **ABOUT TIME!** NOW PERHAPS YOU CAN **RESTORE** THE **HAIR** THAT YOU **CUT OFF** MY WIFE **SIF'S** HEAD AS ONE OF YOUR SO-CALLED **JOKES!**

DON'T **WORRY**, THOR, I'VE ASKED THE **ELVES** AND **DWARVES** TO **SORT** IT OUT...

LOKI ASKS THE ELVES AND DWARVES TO ENTER THE HALL...

MAY I PRESENT THE SONS OF IVALDI – **DVALINN, GRER** AND **BERLING...**

...AND THE BROTHERS **SINDRI** AND **BROKKR!**

ALL HAIL TO THE MIGHTY **ODIN!**

THESE ELVES ARE THE **FINEST CRAFTSMEN** IN ALL SVARTALFHEIM!

STEP FORWARD, **DVALINN!**

FOR THE FAIR LADY SIF, I PRESENT THESE **LOCKS OF PURE GOLD!**

SIMPLY **PLACE** THEM ON YOUR **HEAD** AND ALLOW THE **MAGIC** TO DO ITS **WORK.**

HOW **AMAZING!**

YES, WELL **LEAVE** MY WIFE'S HAIR **ALONE** IN FUTURE, LOKI!

YOU HAVE **REDEEMED** YOURSELF, LOKI!

THAT'S NOT **ALL.** I ALSO ASKED THE ELVES AND DWARVES TO FASHION **GIFTS** FOR **YOU, THOR,** AND **FREYR,** OUR HONORARY AESIR.

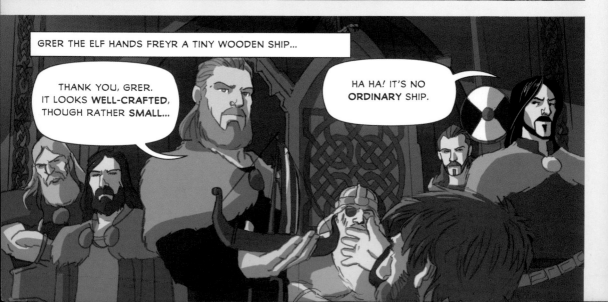

GRER THE ELF HANDS FREYR A TINY WOODEN SHIP...

THANK YOU, GRER. IT LOOKS **WELL-CRAFTED,** THOUGH RATHER **SMALL...**

HA HA! IT'S NO **ORDINARY** SHIP.

AS THE MAGICAL VESSEL SHRINKS DOWN, SINDRI AND BROKKR PUSH FORWARD...

OUR GIFT FOR LORD FREYR IS EVEN BETTER!

A BOAR?

A VERY SPECIAL BOAR. ALONG ITS BACK ARE BRISTLES MADE OF THE FINEST GOLD. THEY WILL LIGHT UP THE DARKEST OF NIGHTS!

AND ITS HIDE IS SO TOUGH, NO WEAPON CAN PIERCE IT. IMAGINE HOW FEARSOME IT WILL BE IN BATTLE!

ODIN IS BECOMING IMPATIENT...

I'M SURE OUR GUEST IS MOST GRATEFUL FOR YOUR PRESENTS. NOW WHAT ABOUT ME?

AH, MY LORD. BROKKR AND I HAVE CRAFTED THIS GOLDEN RING FOR YOU.

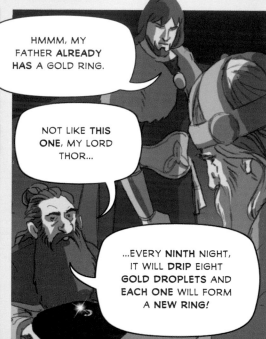

HMMM, MY FATHER ALREADY HAS A GOLD RING.

NOT LIKE THIS ONE, MY LORD THOR...

...EVERY NINTH NIGHT, IT WILL DRIP EIGHT GOLD DROPLETS AND EACH ONE WILL FORM A NEW RING!

EAGER NOT TO BE OUTDONE, BERLING HANDS ODIN A MAGNIFICENT SPEAR...

A GREAT WARRIOR NEEDS A GREAT WEAPON. THIS SPEAR WILL ALWAYS HIT ITS TARGET, NO MATTER HOW FAR AWAY THAT TARGET MAY BE!

THOR DECIDES TO PUT HIS NEW BATTLE HAMMER TO THE TEST...

WHOOSH!

WHAM!

WHOOSH!

WAAAH!

WOOOAH!

HA HA! **THOR'S HAMMER** IS THE **BEST GIFT** OF ALL!

AFTER THE OTHER GODS AGREE WITH ODIN, SINDRI AND BROKKR MARCH UP TO LOKI...

WE **WIN** OUR **BET**, TRICKSTER! PREPARE TO **DIE!**

WHAT'S **GOING ON?**

WE WAGERED THAT OUR GIFT WOULD BE VOTED THE **BEST**. IF WE **WON**, LOKI SAID WE COULD **CUT OFF** HIS **HEAD!**

ER, YES, BUT, UM... I **NEVER** SAID YOU COULD TAKE MY **NECK...**

WHAT?!

...AND THERE'S **NO WAY** YOU CAN **CUT OFF** MY **HEAD** WITHOUT **CUTTING** MY **NECK!**

FUMING WITH FRUSTRATION, SINDRI AND BROKKR PIN LOKI TO THE GROUND AND TAKE OUT NEEDLES AND THREAD...

MOMENTS LATER...

MMMF!

THEY'LL **PAY** FOR THIS **HUMILIATION!**

PERHAPS SPENDING SOME TIME WITH YOUR **LIPS SEALED** WILL TEACH YOU TO USE THEM MORE **WISELY**, LOKI!

WELL SAID, THOR!

HA HA!

HO HO!

It's not long before Thor and Loki put the incident of Sif's hair behind them and go in search of adventure. They head to the fabled giants' stronghold of Utgard in the realm of Jötunheimr.

After flying all day in Thor's chariot, they approach a small hut in the woods at the very edge of Asgard...

GREETINGS, STRANGERS. WE'RE ON OUR WAY TO **UTGARD**. MAY WE **SHELTER HERE** FOR THE NIGHT?

WE'RE **HUMBLE** FOLK, MY LORDS. BUT YOU'RE WELCOME TO **SHARE** WHAT **LITTLE** WE **HAVE**.

THOR AND LOKI JOIN THE COUPLE AND THEIR SON, THIALFI, FOR DINNER...

I'M AFRAID THIS **VEGETABLE SOUP** IS RATHER **THIN**, MY LORDS.

NOT TO WORRY, MADAM. I THINK I CAN PROVIDE US WITH SOMETHING **BETTER**...

THOR LEAVES THE HUT AND RETURNS A FEW MINUTES LATER WITH THE CARCASSES OF THE GOATS THAT PULL HIS CHARIOT...

YOU'VE **SLAUGHTERED TOOTH-GRINDER** AND **TOOTH-BARER!**

HOW WILL WE CONTINUE OUR JOURNEY **NOW?**

DON'T **WORRY**, LOKI.

PLEASE COOK THESE ANIMALS, MADAM. BUT **SAVE** THEIR **SKINS** AND **KEEP** EVERY **BONE** INTACT.

THE GOATS ARE PREPARED AND SOON THE POOR PEASANTS ARE ENJOYING THE FINEST MEAL THEY'VE TASTED IN A LONG TIME...

THE NEXT MORNING...

THANK YOU FOR YOUR **HOSPITALITY**. NOW MY COMPANION AND I MUST BE ON OUR WAY.

I SUPPOSE WE'LL HAVE TO **WALK** TO **UTGARD** NOW?

NOT AT ALL. SINCE I RECEIVED **MJÖLNIR**, I'VE DISCOVERED IT'S **MORE THAN JUST** A **WEAPON**...

BUT YOUNG THIALFI IGNORES THOR'S INSTRUCTIONS AND SNAPS A BONE TO SUCK ON THE TASTY MARROW INSIDE...

THOR TAKES THE GOATS' SKINS AND BONES AND WAVES HIS MAGICAL HAMMER OVER THEM...

BAAH!

BAAH!

I DON'T **BELIEVE IT!**

BUT TOOTH-GRINDER IS WALKING LAMELY...

ONE OF THE **BONES** MUST HAVE BEEN **BROKEN!**

I CONFESS THAT WAS **ME**. I BEG **FORGIVENESS**, MY LORD!

AS YOUR FAMILY WERE **KIND** TO US, I WON'T **PUNISH** YOU. INSTEAD I MERELY ASK THAT YOU BECOME MY **SERVANT.**

WITHOUT TWO FIT GOATS TO PULL THE CHARIOT, THOR AND HIS PARTY CONTINUE THEIR JOURNEY ON FOOT. LEAVING TOOTH-GRINDER WITH THE PEASANTS TO RECOVER (ALONG WITH TOOTH-BARER), THOR, LOKI AND THIALFI SET OFF...

GOODBYE MY SON!

CARRYING A BAG OF PROVISIONS FROM THIALFI'S PARENTS, THE EXPLORERS LEAVE ASGARD. BY DUSK THEY ARE WELL INTO THE REALM OF JÖTUNHEIMR...

WE MUST **LOOK AROUND** FOR SOMEWHERE TO SPEND THE **NIGHT.**

IT'S NOT LONG BEFORE THEY COME UPON A HUGE, STRANGELY SHAPED BUILDING...

LET'S GO **INSIDE.** BUT BE ON YOUR **GUARD!**

I'VE NEVER SEEN A **HALL** LIKE *THIS* BEFORE!

THE MASSIVE ENTRANCE LEADS TO FIVE SNAKING CORRIDORS...

THE PLACE SEEMS **DESERTED.** WE'LL SPEND THE NIGHT IN ONE OF THESE **TUNNELS.**

THAT NIGHT, THOR AND THE OTHERS ARE WOKEN BY A FURIOUS EARTHQUAKE...

WHAT'S **THAT?**

I'M **SCARED!**

KEEP **CALM!** WHATEVER IT IS, I HAVE **MJÖLNIR** TO **PROTECT** US.

THE EXPLORERS SPEND A TREMULOUS, SLEEPLESS NIGHT...

THE NEXT MORNING, WITH THE GROUND STILL TREMBLING, THOR AND HIS COMPANIONS CAUTIOUSLY LEAVE THE STRANGE HALL...

THERE DOESN'T SEEM TO BE ANY **DAMAGE** OUT HERE!

BUT **WHAT'S** CAUSING THESE TERRIBLE **VIBRATIONS?**

THE ANSWER BECOMES ALL TOO CLEAR WHEN THEY REACH HIGHER GROUND...

LOOK!

ZZZZZ!
A GIANT! AND HE'S THE SIZE OF A MOUNTAIN!
IT WASN'T A HALL WE SLEPT IN LAST NIGHT. IT WAS ONE OF THIS CREATURE'S GLOVES!

AT THAT MOMENT, THE GIANT SUDDENLY WAKES FROM HIS SLUMBER...

WELL, WELL. AN AUDIENCE OF **LITTLE PEOPLE**, COME TO **GREET** ME!

I AM **THOR** OF THE **AESIR**. I MAY BE **SMALLER** THAN YOU, BUT I **WARN** YOU THAT I CAN **DEFEND** MYSELF AND MY COMPANIONS!

MY NAME IS **SKRYMIR** AND I MEAN YOU **NO HARM**. WHAT **BRINGS** YOU TO THE **LAND OF GIANTS**?

WE JOURNEY IN SEARCH OF **UTGARD**.

I'M ON MY WAY **EAST**, BUT I CAN LEAD YOU PART OF THE WAY TO **UTGARD**. LET ME LIGHTEN YOUR LOAD BY CARRYING YOUR **PROVISIONS** IN MY **SACK**.

THOR AGREES, AND THEY TRAVEL ON WITH THEIR NEW COMPANION...

THAT NIGHT, THEY STOP TO REST IN A FOREST. SKRYMIR QUICKLY FALLS ASLEEP. BUT WHEN THOR GOES TO TAKE THE PROVISIONS FROM THE GIANT'S SACK...

HURRY UP, THOR! WE'RE **STARVING**.

GNNNN! I CAN'T **UNTIE** THE **WRETCHED** THING!

FRUSTRATED AND HUNGRY, THOR DEALS THE SNORING GIANT A POWERFUL BLOW WITH HIS HAMMER...

WHACK!

THOR'S ACTIONS BRIEFLY WAKE SKRYMIR. BUT HE SEEMS QUITE UNTROUBLED...

YAWN! DID A LEAF FALL ON MY HEAD? ZZZZZZZ...

THAT NIGHT, THE GIANT'S LOUD SNORING KEEPS HIS COMPANIONS AWAKE...

ZZZ ZZZ!

NOT **AGAIN**!

I'M NOT **STANDING** FOR **THIS**!

THOR CLIMBS ONTO THE GIANT AND HITS HIM EVEN HARDER THAN BEFORE...

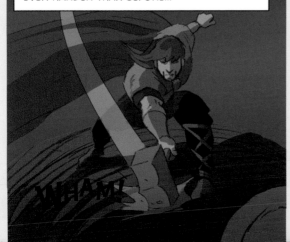

WHAM!

BUT...

HMMMM... WAS THAT A FALLING **ACORN**? ZZZZZZZ...

UTGARD-LOKI TURNS TO THIALFI...

AND WHAT **SKILLS** DOES THE **LITTLE SERVANT** OF THOR POSSESS?

WELL, I'VE NEVER MET **ANYONE** WHO CAN **OUTRUN** ME!

AND SO THE NEXT CONTEST IS DECIDED – A RACE BETWEEN THIALFI AND UTGARD-LOKI'S SERVANT, HUGI, ACROSS A NEARBY PLAIN...

FIRST ONE TO THE **LONE PINE** AND BACK IS THE **WINNER!**

GOOD LUCK, THIALFI!

HUGI MAY BE **BIGGER** THAN YOU, BUT YOU'RE MORE **AGILE!**

THIALFI AND HUGI STAND POISED AT THE START LINE...

GO!

AT FIRST, THE NIMBLE THIALFI HAS THE EDGE ON HIS BULKY OPPONENT...

COME ON, THIALFI!

HE'S REACHED THE TREE **FIRST**!

BUT ONCE HUGI HAS GATHERED MOMENTUM, HE CATCHES UP WITH THIALFI...

...AND OVERTAKES HIM...

THE **WINNER**!

EVERYONE RETURNS TO THE HALL, WHERE THOR FINALLY RECEIVES HIS OWN CHALLENGE FROM UTGARD-LOKI...

LET'S SEE IF YOU CAN DO **BETTER** THAN YOUR **LITTLE FRIENDS**...

...DOWN **ALL** THE **ALE** IN THIS **DRINKING HORN** IN **ONE** ATTEMPT!

SIMPLE!

THOR RAISES THE HORN TO HIS LIPS AND DRINKS DEEPLY...

GLUG, GLUG, GLUG!

A MINUTE PASSES, BUT TO THOR'S BEWILDERMENT...

SURELY THERE CAN'T ANY **MORE** ALE IN HERE? IT JUST **KEEPS COMING!**

HIS LUNGS BURSTING, THOR CAN ONLY LAST ANOTHER MINUTE BEFORE...

GASP! CHOKE!

HA HA! IT SEEMS THE GREAT GOD OF **THUNDER** HAS RUN OUT OF **PUFF!**

PERHAPS HE NEEDS A **SIMPLER** TASK...

UTGARD-LOKI LEADS EVERYONE INTO A SIDE CHAMBER...

LET'S SEE IF YOU CAN **LIFT UP** MY PET **CAT**...

...I KNOW HE'S RATHER LARGER THAT YOU'RE USED TO, BUT IT SHOULD BE **SIMPLE ENOUGH**, **EVEN** FOR **YOU**!

THE TASK SEEMS SUSPICIOUSLY EASY, SO THOR GRASPS THE CAT WITH CONFIDENCE...

BUT...

GNNNNNN! HOW CAN **ONE**... CAT... BE SO... **HEAVY**?

AFTER STRUGGLING WITH THE ANIMAL FOR SOME TIME, THOR ONLY MANAGES TO GET A SINGLE PAW OFF THE GROUND...

HNNNGH!

BEFORE CONCEDING DEFEAT...

GASP!

THAT WAS NO **ORDINARY** CAT!

COME NOW, LET'S NOT HAVE **EXCUSES**!

I'LL GIVE YOU ONE **LAST** CHANCE TO SUGGEST A CHALLENGE!

I'M A **WARRIOR**, UTGARD-LOKI. I'LL **WRESTLE** YOU OR ANY OF YOUR SUBJECTS TO THE **GROUND**!

VERY WELL, BUT **MOST** OF THEM WOULD BE **INSULTED** TO WRESTLE SOMEONE SO **PUNY**...

...I KNOW, YOU SHALL WRESTLE ELLI, MY **OLD NURSE**!

I DON'T FIGHT **OLD WOMEN**, GIANT!

I THINK YOU'LL BE **SURPRISED** AT HER **STRENGTH**. UNLESS OF COURSE, YOU'RE **AFRAID**?

HIS PRIDE AT STAKE, THOR SQUARES UP TO THE OLD WOMAN...

...AND GRASPS HER TIGHTLY AROUND HER FRAIL SHOULDERS...

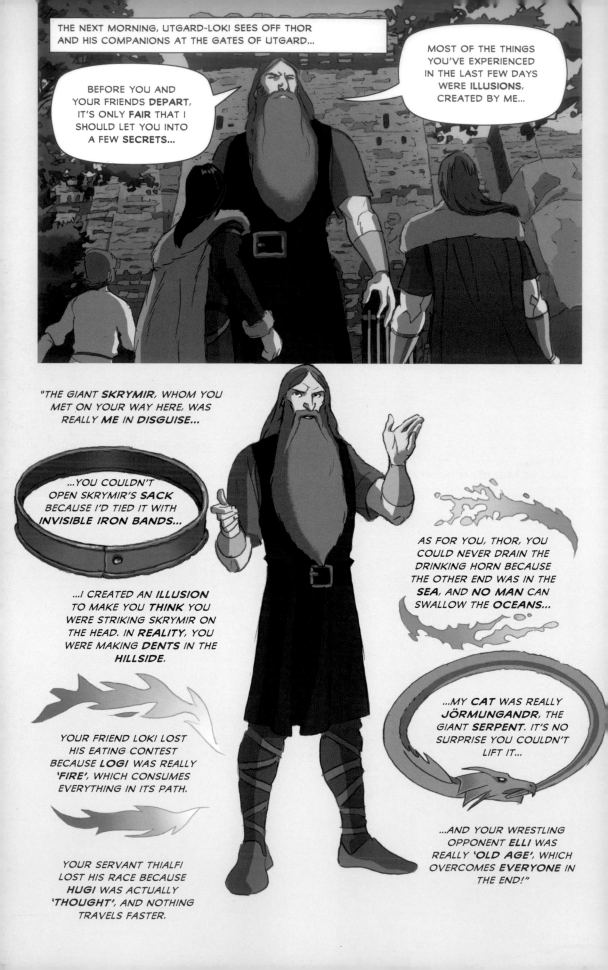

I'LL ADMIT HE'S A **FINE-LOOKING** BEAST. BUT STILL NOT A PATCH ON **MY HORSE GULLFAXI!**

EVEN YOUR **EIGHT-LEGGED** STEED COULDN'T OUTRUN **HIM!**

YOU **THINK SO?** I'LL WAGER **NO HORSE** IN **ALL** OF JÖTUNHEIMR COULD **BEAT** SLEIPNIR!

VERY WELL! MY NAME IS **HRUNGNIR** AND I ACCEPT YOUR **CHALLENGE.** LET'S SEE HOW YOU AND THAT **FREAKISH** HORSE OF YOURS FARE AGAINST A GIANT!

GULLFAXI ANSWERS HIS MASTER'S WHISTLE, THE GIANT MOUNTS THE MASSIVE HORSE, AND THE RACE IS ON...

THE SNAKING MOUNTAIN PATHS ARE VERY FAMILIAR TO HRUNGNIR, AND HE SOON OVERTAKES HIS RIVAL...

HA HA! SO MUCH FOR THE MIGHTY ALLFATHER!

THE RIDERS HURTLE DOWN THE MOUNTAIN TRACK, UNTIL IT COMES TO AN END AT THE EDGE OF A CLIFF...

LOOKS LIKE YOU'VE LOST, ODIN. I'LL EASILY REACH THE CLIFF EDGE BEFORE YOU!

BUT ODIN REMAINS CONFIDENT...

WHO SAID THE RACE MUST END HERE?

ODIN MAKES NO ATTEMPT TO SLOW DOWN AS HE APPROACHES THE CLIFF EDGE...

...AND HRUNGNIR CAN ONLY LOOK ON IN BEMUSEMENT...

THEN, TO THE GIANT'S AMAZEMENT...

LET'S SEE YOUR NAG DO *THIS!*

CRAZY WITH FRUSTRATION, HRUNGNIR URGES HIS HORSE OVER THE CLIFF EDGE...

RAAAAAH!

SPLASH!

FOR A MOMENT, ODIN THINKS HE'S SEEN THE LAST OF THE BOASTFUL GIANT, BUT THEN...

SPLUTTER! I DON'T GIVE UP *THAT* EASILY, OLD MAN!

WHOOSH!

THE RIDERS URGE THEIR MOUNTS ON, EACH ONE DESPERATE TO WIN...

FASTER, GULLFAXI!

GIDDY UP, SLEIPNIR!

JUST AS THE GIANT LOOKS CERTAIN TO SECURE VICTORY, ODIN'S HORSE PULLS AHEAD...

RAAAGH!

I'VE WON!

THOR AND HIS FELLOW AESIR GATHER AROUND TO HEAR ABOUT THE RACE...

HA! I WOULD HAVE BEATEN THE OLD MAN EASILY IF HE HADN'T CHEATED BY FLYING HALF THE WAY...

...AND NOW HE'S TRICKED ME INTO YOUR STRONGHOLD SO HE MAY KEEP ME PRISONER!

YOU RODE WELL, ALLFATHER!

COME NOW, HRUNGNIR, BE A GOOD SPORT AND I'LL ALLOW YOU TO GO. AGREE IT WAS A FAIR WIN AND YOU MAY EVEN JOIN OUR CELEBRATORY FEAST!

THE GIANT GRUDGINGLY ACCEPTS ODIN'S OFFER AND THAT NIGHT TAKES HIS PLACE NEXT TO THOR AT THE FEAST...

THE LADY FREYA AND MY **WIFE** SIF WILL KEEP YOUR **PLATE** PILED **HIGH** AND YOUR **CUP OVERFLOWING** WITH **MEAD**!

LET **NO ONE** SAY THE **AESIR** AREN'T **GENEROUS** HOSTS!

BUT AS THE NIGHT WEARS ON, HRUNGNIR QUICKLY BECOMES LOUDER AND ROWDIER, MUCH TO THOR'S ANNOYANCE...

THIS IS A **FINE HALL**. I THINK I'LL CARRY THE **WHOLE PLACE** BACK TO **JÖTUNHEIMR**!

IT WOULD LOOK EVEN **BETTER** THERE!

HAVE A **CARE**, WHAT YOU **SAY**, GIANT!

I'D **KILL** ALL THE **AESIR** FIRST, OF COURSE. ALL EXCEPT **YOUR WIFE**. I'D TAKE HER AS **MY OWN**!

YOU INSULT MY **HOME** AND MY **LADY**! I **CHALLENGE** YOU TO A **DUEL**!

THE GIANT'S WEAPON IS SHATTERED, BUT THE IMPACT OF THE BLOW SENDS A SHARD OF RAZOR SHARP STONE FLYING AT THOR...

OOOWW!

HRUNGNIR REELS AND SWAYS, FATALLY INJURED BY THOR'S HAMMER BLOW...

STILL IN SHOCK FROM HIS OWN WOUND, THOR IS ONLY JUST COMING TO HIS SENSES WHEN HE SEES THE DYING GIANT TOPPLING TOWARDS HIM...

GRAAAGH!

RUN THOR, RUN!

NONSENSE! SIF IS AS **LOYAL** TO **ME** AS THE **SUN** IS TO THE **SKY**!

THAT'S NOT THE **WORST** OF IT. WHEN YOU GET HOME, YOU'LL FIND YOUR **MOTHER DEAD**!

NO! I **CAN'T** BELIEVE IT! I **WON'T** BELIEVE IT!

IF YOU WEREN'T SO **OLD**, I'D **STRIKE** YOU **DOWN** FOR YOUR **LIES**!

HA! SO THE '**BRAVE**' THOR IS JUST A **COWARD** AFTER ALL!

A **COWARD?** WHY I'LL HAVE YOU KNOW I ONCE **KILLED** A **MIGHT'Y STONE GIANT** FROM JÖTUNHEIMR...

JUST THE **ONE?** BY THE TIME I WAS **YOUR AGE**, I'D KILLED **FIFTY**!

OH YES? WELL, I ONCE DEFEATED THE **SHE-WOLVES** OF THE ISLE OF HLESEY WHO **CRUSHED** MY **SHIP** AND **ATTACKED** ME WITH **IRON CLUBS**!

HA! I WOULD HAVE **CHARMED** THEM WITH MY **WIT**, AS I DO **ALL WOMEN**!

I'VE HEARD **ENOUGH** OF YOUR **LIES** AND EMPTY **BOASTS**.

IF **YOU** WON'T TAKE ME **ACROSS** THE **RIVER**, I SHALL FIND MY **OWN** WAY!

THOR TRUDGES THE LENGTH OF THE RIVER IN SEARCH OF A STRETCH THAN CAN BE BRIDGED...

HOW **DARE** THAT **ROGUE** TELL SUCH BARE-FACED **LIES!**

BUT THE FURTHER HE WALKS, THE MORE THOR BEGINS TO DOUBT HIS OWN CONVICTIONS...

WHAT IF HE **WASN'T** LYING, THOUGH?

HE SEEMED TO **KNOW** ME, THOUGH I'D NEVER **SET EYES** ON THE FELLOW **BEFORE...**

...SURELY MY BELOVED **SIF** WOULDN'T **RUN OFF** WITH A **MORTAL?**

MY MOTHER WAS **SAFE** AND **WELL** WHEN I LEFT ASGARD. BUT WHAT IF SHE'S **SUDDENLY** FALLEN ILL?

SOON THOR IS PLAGUED BY FEAR AND DESPERATE TO REACH HOME...

AT **LAST!** A WAY ACROSS!

HAVING WALKED FAR OUT OF HIS WAY, IT IS MANY HOURS LATER BEFORE AN ANXIOUS THOR FINALLY RUSHES INTO THE HALL OF BILSKIRNIR, HIS FAMILY HOME...

THIALFI! WHERE ARE **SIF** AND MY **MOTHER?**

TELL ME THEY'RE **HERE!** TELL ME THEY'RE **SAFE!**

A few months later, intense preparations are under way at Asgard for a great feast. Thor finds himself summoned to the hall of Valaskjálf by his father...

I HAVE A **MISSION** FOR YOU, MY SON...

...VISIT THE **SEA GOD AEGIR** AND ASK HIM TO BREW ENOUGH **MEAD** FOR OUR **FEAST**.

AS YOU **COMMAND**, ALLFATHER.

THOR VISITS AEGIR AND PASSES ON ODIN'S REQUEST...

I COULD CERTAINLY BREW ENOUGH **MEAD** FOR **ALL** THE **AESIR**, BUT I DON'T POSSESS A **CAULDRON** *BIG* ENOUGH TO **PUT IT IN**!

A FRUSTRATED THOR RETURNS HOME AND CONFIDES HIS PROBLEM TO TÝR...

HMMM. MY FATHER, **HYMIR THE GIANT**, OWNS A *MASSIVE* CAULDRON...

A **GIANT'S** CAULDRON SHOULD BE *MORE* THAN **BIG ENOUGH** FOR OUR NEEDS!

YES, THOUGH I SHOULD **WARN** YOU THAT **HYMIR** IS **NOT** KNOWN FOR HIS **GOOD TEMPER**!

THOR DOESN'T HAVE LONG TO WAIT BEFORE HE FEELS A SHARP TUG AT THE LINE...

WOOAH!

HIS MUSCLES STRAINING, THOR SLOWLY HEAVES THE LINE OUT OF THE WAVES...

... I'VE...

LET'S SEE...

...WHAT...

HIS LUNGS BURSTING, THOR SWIMS BACK TO THE SHIP TOWING THE THRASHING SEA SERPENT BEHIND HIM...

WITH ONE LAST EFFORT, THOR HAULS HIMSELF BACK ONTO THE BOAT, PULLING THE SERPENT WITH HIM...

GNNNRR!

YOU CAN'T **BRING** THAT **BEAST** ANY **CLOSER.** IT'LL **KILL** US!

I'M **CUTTING** THE LINE!

NO!

...WHO GATHERS SUPPORT FROM HIS FELLOW GIANTS EN ROUTE...

GRAAAGH!

YAAAARH!

RAAAAAGHH!

WEIGHED DOWN BY THE MASSIVE CAULDRON, THOR DECIDES TO STOP AND FIGHT...

...AND THAT!

WHAM!

BANG!

CRACK!

TAKE THAT!

...AND THAT!

HYMIR EVENTUALLY CONCEDES DEFEAT...

TAKE MY POT FOR YOUR WRETCHED MEAD, THEN. I HOPE IT CHOKES YOU!

...AND THE GODS RETURN TO ASGARD...

...WHERE HYMIR'S CAULDRON IS PUT TO GOOD USE AT A FABULOUS FEAST...

THREE CHEERS FOR THOR!

A few days later, Thor is preparing for a raiding expedition. But when he goes to fetch his war hammer Mjölnir from its usual place in his hall…

IT'S **GONE!** **MJÖLNIR** IS **GONE!**

ARE YOU **CERTAIN,** MY LOVE?

OF **COURSE** I'M **CERTAIN,** SIF!

BUT **WHO** COULD HAVE **TAKEN** IT?

I'LL **WAGER** IT'S THAT FOOL **LOKI,** UP TO HIS USUAL STUPID **TRICKS!**

THOR STORMS INTO LOKI'S ROOMS AND DEMANDS AN EXPLANATION…

I DON'T KNOW **WHAT** YOU'RE **TALKING** ABOUT, THOR! I **DIDN'T** TAKE YOUR HAMMER, I **SWEAR!**

HMMM. WELL YOU CAN *PROVE* THAT BY **HELPING** ME TO **FIND** IT!

LOKI RELUCTANTLY AGREES AND PAYS A VISIT TO FREYR'S SISTER, FREYA…

DON'T **TELL ME,** YOU WANT TO **BORROW** MY **FALCON CLOAK** AGAIN?

THOR WANTS ME TO SEARCH FOR HIS MISSING **HAMMER,** MY GUESS IS A **GIANT** STOLE IT, SO I NEED TO **FLY** TO **JÖTUNHEIMR.**

LOKI WRAPS FREYA'S MAGICAL GARMENT AROUND HIMSELF AND IS TRANSFORMED INTO...

...A FALCON!

IN HIS NEW GUISE, LOKI SOARS INTO THE AIR AND TRAVELS TO JÖTUNHEIMR...

HE SPENDS THE NEXT FEW DAYS SPYING ON EVERY GIANT HE SEES AND LISTENING IN ON THEIR CONVERSATIONS...

HAVING LEARNED NOTHING OF THOR'S HAMMER, LOKI IS ABOUT TO GIVE UP WHEN HE SEES TWO SERVANTS OUTSIDE THE PALACE OF THRYMR, KING OF THE FROST GIANTS...

WHEW! I'M **EXHAUSTED!** THAT **HOLE** WE **DUG** MUST HAVE BEEN **OVER TWENTY MILES** DEEP!

WELL, THOSE WERE **KING THRYMR'S** ORDERS. THERE'S **NO WAY** ANY AESIR WILL FIND THAT **HAMMER** NOW!

I **KNEW** IT! TIME I HAD A WORD WITH **KING THRYMR!**

HOW **FLATTERING!** COME, MY LOVE, LET ME **KISS** YOU!

OH NO!

LUCKILY FOR THOR, THRYMR PULLS BACK...

I DIDN'T EXPECT YOUR **EYES** TO BE SO **BLOODSHOT,** MY LOVE!

ER, WELL YOU SEE, THE LADY FREYA HAS BEEN **SO LOOKING FORWARD** TO THE **WEDDING,** SHE **HASN'T SLEPT** FOR EIGHT NIGHTS!

BEFORE THRYMR CAN TAKE ANOTHER LOOK AT HIS NEW BRIDE, HE IS INTERRUPTED BY THE ARRIVAL OF HIS SERVANTS...

WE'VE BROUGHT THE **AESIR WAR HAMMER** AS YOU COMMANDED, YOUR MAJESTY!

AT **LAST!**

WITHOUT HESITATING, THOR LEAPS FROM HIS SEAT AND GRABS MJÖLNIR...

I THINK YOU'LL FIND THIS IS **MY** PROPERTY!

WHAT?

OWWWW!

WHACK!

Loki can't resist the urge to cause more trouble among the giants. A few days later, he borrows Freya's magic cloak and once again transforms himself into a falcon.

Soon he is swooping over Geirrödsgard, home of Geirröd the giant...

I'LL FLY DOWN AND *SPY* ON THE *GIANTS* HERE.

HE PERCHES ON A WIDOW LEDGE AND PEERS INTO THE HALL WHERE GEIRRÖD AND HIS TWO SPOILED DAUGHTERS, GJÁLP AND GREIP, ARE FEASTING...

BUT LOKI HASN'T BEEN THERE LONG, WHEN...

WHAT A **FINE BIRD**, FATHER! I **WANT** IT!

NO, *I* SAW IT FIRST. *I* WANT IT!

YOU SHALL *BOTH* HAVE IT.

CATCH THAT **BIRD** FOR MY **DAUGHTERS!**

AS YOU **COMMAND**, LORD GEIRRÖD.

BY THE TIME THOR ARRIVES IN THE MOUNTAINOUS REALM OF JÖTUNHEIMR, THE WEATHER HAS TAKEN A TURN FOR THE WORSE...

I'LL TAKE **SHELTER** IN THAT **CAVE** FOR THE NIGHT.

WHEN HE ENTERS...

IT LOOKS LIKE THE PLACE IS **ALREADY** INHABITED.

THOR'S SUSPICIONS ARE SOON CONFIRMED...

THUMP!
THUMP!
THUMP!

SOMETHING'S **COMING!**

WHO ARE YOU?

I AM **THOR** OF THE **AESIR!**

SO YOU'RE THE INFAMOUS **SON** OF **ODIN**. MY NAME'S **GRITHR**. ODIN AND I WERE VERY **CLOSE** ONCE.

PLEASE MAKE YOURSELF **COMFORTABLE** WHILE I PREPARE US BOTH A **MEAL**.

AS THEY EAT, THOR TELLS GRITHR ABOUT HIS PLAN TO FIGHT GEIRRÖD...

IT WON'T BE AN **EASY TASK** TO DEFEAT GEIRRÖD WITHOUT **SOME** PROTECTION.

I'VE **VOWED** NOT TO USE MY **MAGICAL WEAPON** AGAINST HIM.

BUT YOU *COULD* USE WEAPONS CRAFTED BY **ME**! HERE, TAKE THIS **BELT**, **STAFF** AND **IRON GLOVES**.

THANK YOU, GRITHR!

AT FIRST LIGHT, ARMED WITH GRITHR'S GIFTS, THOR SETS OFF FOR GEIRRÖD'S HALL...

FAREWELL, THOR, AND **GOOD FORTUNE***!*

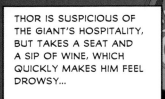

THOR IS SUSPICIOUS OF THE GIANT'S HOSPITALITY, BUT TAKES A SEAT AND A SIP OF WINE, WHICH QUICKLY MAKES HIM FEEL DROWSY...

HMM, GEIRRÖD IS **UP** TO SOMETHING. BUT... **WHAT**... I... WONDER... ZZZZZZ!

THOR DOZES OFF AND LATER WAKES WITH A START TO FEEL HIS CHAIR RISING INTO THE AIR...

WOOOOAH!

THOR FINDS HIMSELF CLIMBING HIGHER AND HIGHER...

WHAT GIANTS' SORCERY IS THIS?

HE LOOKS UPWARDS IN HORROR...

IF I DON'T **STOP** THIS THING, I'LL BE **CRUSHED** AGAINST THE CEILING!

THINKING QUICKLY, THOR WEDGES GRITHR'S POWERFUL STAFF BETWEEN HIMSELF AND THE CEILING...

WHAM!

For many years, Thor and the rest of the Aesir continue their adventurous lives, unaware that the end is so near at hand.

But their world is suddenly torn apart by the turmoil of Ragnarok – the destruction of the gods...

RAGNAROK BEGINS WITH THE 'GREAT WINTER' WHICH LASTS FOR THREE, BITTERLY COLD YEARS.

WARS BREAK OUT ACROSS THE NINE REALMS. IN MIDGARD, EVERYONE IS KILLED EXCEPT FOR A COUPLE NAMED LÍF AND LÍFTHRASIR WHO TAKE REFUGE IN THE BRANCHES OF YGGDRASIL...

IN ASGARD, LOKI FALLS OUT WITH THE AESIR AND TRAVELS TO NIFLHEIM, THE REALM OF THE DEAD, WHERE HE MUSTERS AN ARMY...

THE **AESIR** WILL **PAY** FOR NOT TREATING ME WITH MORE **RESPECT!**

MEANWHILE, THE TERRIBLE WOLVES SKÖLL AND HATI SWALLOW THE SUN...

...AND THE MOON...

BUT LIFE IS NOT TOTALLY EXTINGUISHED.

AFTER THE FIRES HAVE BURNED THEMSELVES OUT, A NEW, FERTILE WORLD EMERGES...

...AND SOMEHOW A FEW BEINGS SURVIVE THE CARNAGE, INCLUDING THE MORTALS LÍF AND LÍFTHRASIR WHO MUST BEGIN THE TASK OF RE-POPULATING THE EARTH...

A HANDFUL OF GODS SURVIVE TOO, INCLUDING THOR'S GROWN UP SONS MAGNI AND MÓDI...

WE MUST DO JUSTICE BY OUR **FATHER** AND THE REST OF THE **FALLEN AESIR**.

LET'S BUILD A NEW, **PEACEFUL** REALM, **HERE** ON THIS **PLAIN** WHERE **ASGARD** ONCE STOOD.

A GLINT OF SILVER ON THE GROUND CATCHES MÓDI'S EYE...

WHAT'S **THAT**?

MAGNI BENDS DOWN AND SCRAPES THE EARTH AWAY FROM THE HALF-BURIED OBJECT...

IT **CAN'T** BE, **CAN** IT?

IT **IS!**

THE END

The Story of
THOR

The character of Thor is most closely associated with the Norse mythology of ancient and medieval Scandinavia. The people living there were related to the Germanic tribes of what is now Luxembourg, Belgium, Poland, Austria, Northern France, the Netherlands and Germany.

Hercules

The earliest known references to the character of Thor appear in Roman literature, where he and the other gods of the Germanic people were reinterpreted as existing Roman deities. In these works, Thor was referred to either as Jupiter or Hercules, possibly because Thor's fantastic hammer was similar to Hercules's powerful club.

An early Germanic version of the name Thor features as part of an inscription on a 7th century brooch where it appears as 'Donar'. There are also mentions of 'Thunor' in Old English texts of the 8th century and, in a 9th century manuscript, 'Thunaer' is referred to as an Old Saxon god.

In the 10th century, an Icelandic writer named Eilífr Goðrúnarson wrote a poem called *Thorsdrapa* which tells the story of Thor's battle with Geirröd the giant.

In the 11th century, the German chronicler Adam of Bremen wrote about a temple in Uppsala, Sweden, that contained a statue of Thor. The locals believed he was a god who had the power to control thunder, lightning, winds, storms and fertility.

However, most of our knowledge of the adventures of Thor comes from two sources – the *Poetic Edda* and the *Prose Edda*.

The *Poetic Edda* is a collection of Old Norse poems whose original authors are unknown because the tales were passed on by word of mouth. It was compiled in the 13th century by an Icelandic priest and scholar named Sæmund Sigfússon. Of the book's thirty-two chapters, Thor features most prominently in six.

Sæmund Sigfússon

In *Voluspa* (*The Prophecy of the Volva*) a volva, a foreteller of the future, informs Odin about Ragnarok, the battle at the end of the world, which will see Thor defeated by Jörmungandr, the world-encircling serpent.

In *Hárbarðsljóð* (*The Lay of Harbard*) [a 'lay' was a poem intended to be sung] Thor encounters a ferryman, who may possibly be Odin in disguise. The pair proceed to trade insults as they attempt to outdo each other's exploits.

Hymiskviða (*Hymir's Poem*) tells the story of Thor's mission to collect a giant cauldron from Hymir the giant, in the course of which he almost catches Jörmungandr.

In *Lokasenna* (*Loki's Quarrel*), Loki insults the gods and Thor threatens to knock off Loki's head with his hammer, Mjölnir, if he doesn't stop.

Alviss

Þrymskviða (*The Lay of Thrymr*) recounts the theft of Mjölnir by the giant Thrymr. In order to retrieve the hammer, Thor must disguise himself as the goddess Freya and take part in a wedding ceremony.

Finally, *Alvíssmál* (*The Talk of Alviss*) sees a dwarf named Alviss claiming Thor's daughter for his bride. When Thor refuses, a verbal battle of wits ensues.

The *Prose Edda* is a collection of Norse legends and history, believed to have been compiled by Icelandic scholar Snorri Sturluson in the early 13th century.

In the prologue, Sturluson suggests that Thor was based on a real prince of the city of Troy in Asia Minor (modern Turkey). He goes on to claim that Thor's descendants made their way to Scandinavia and that the origin of the word 'Aesir' is 'men from Asia' and 'Asgard' comes from 'Asian city'.

Thor's major appearance in the *Prose Edda* comes in the chapter entitled *Skáldskaparmál* (*The Language of Poetry*) which features a retelling of Eilífr Goðrúnarson's story of Thor's battle with Geirröd the giant.

Thor was one of the most beloved Norse gods, as he was the patron of all free men and women and took care of the majority of the population.

Thor and his adventures have been the inspiration for many works of art over the years, including Henry Fuseli's *Thor Battering the Midgard Serpent* (1790) and Mårten Eskil Winge's *Thor's Fight with the Giants* (1872). Thor has also featured in many poems, including part of *The Saga of King Olaf* by Henry Wadsworth Longfellow (1863).

Stan Lee, Larry Lieber and Jack Kirby created a superhero named Thor Odinson who first appeared in Marvel Comics' *Journey into Mystery* in 1962. Since then, the character has gone on to appear in numerous comic books, both individually and as a founding member of Marvel's superhero team the Avengers. From 2011 onwards, Marvel's Thor has been portrayed in many big budget Hollywood movies including *Thor*, *Thor: The Dark World* and *Thor: Ragnarok*, as well as films featuring the Avengers.

From the mists of ancient mythology to the hi-tech 21st century, Thor, armed with his trusty war hammer, Mjölnir, has captured the imaginations of generations, and looks set to continue to do so.

Thor

Russell Punter was born in Bedfordshire, England. From an early age he enjoyed writing and illustrating his own stories. He trained as a graphic designer at art college in West Sussex before entering publishing in 1987. He has written over sixty books for children, ranging from original stories to adaptations of classic novels.

Andrea da Rold was born in Milan, Italy. He graduated from Milan's prestigious Academy of Fine Arts, and he still lives in the city today. He works as a cartoonist for Star Comics (*Samuel Sand*, *Lazarus Ledd*) and as an illustrator of children's books, working with, among others, Mondadori, De Agostini and Giunti. He illustrates the covers of the very popular *Geronimo Stilton* for Piemme and collaborates on Mondadori's *Focus Jr.* magazine.

Dr. Anne Millard has been writing and consulting on historical books for children of all ages since she left university. As well as a B.A. Hons. from London University, she has diplomas in education and archaeology, along with a Ph.D. in Egyptology.

Mike Collins has been creating comics for over 25 years. Starting on *Spider-Man* and *Transformers* for Marvel UK, he has also worked for DC, 2000AD and a host of other publishers. In that time he's written or drawn almost all the major characters for each company – *Wonder Woman*, *Batman*, *Superman*, *Flash*, *Teen Titans*, *X-Men*, *Captain Britain*, *Judge Dredd*, *Sláine*, *Rogue Trooper*, *Darkstars*, *Peter Cannon: Thunderbolt* and more. He currently draws a series of noir crime fiction graphic novels, *Varg Veum*. He also provides storyboards for TV and movies, including *Doctor Who*, *Sherlock*, *Igam Ogam*, *Claude*, *Hana's Helpline* and *Horrid Henry*.

Cover design: Matt Preston

First published in 2019 by Usborne Publishing Ltd., Usborne House, 83–85 Saffron Hill, London ECIN 8RT England. www.usborne.com Copyright © 2019 Usborne Publishing Ltd. The name Usborne and the devices ♀ ⊕ are Trade Marks of Usborne Publishing Ltd. All rights reserved. No part of this publication may be reproduced, stored in a retrieval system, or transmitted in any form or by any means, electronic, mechanical, photocopying, recording or otherwise without the prior permission of Usborne Publishing Ltd. First published in America 2019. UE. EDC, Tulsa, Oklahoma 74146 www.usbornebooksandmore.com Library of Congress Control Number: 2019944912